6-28-01

For Christine,

Who can tell

the future

Love

Stephen

N A N C Y   W I L L A R D

The Tale I Told Sasha

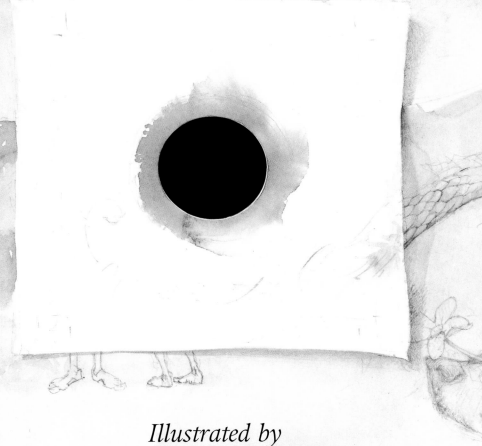

Illustrated by

David Christiana

Little, Brown and Company
BOSTON   NEW YORK   LONDON

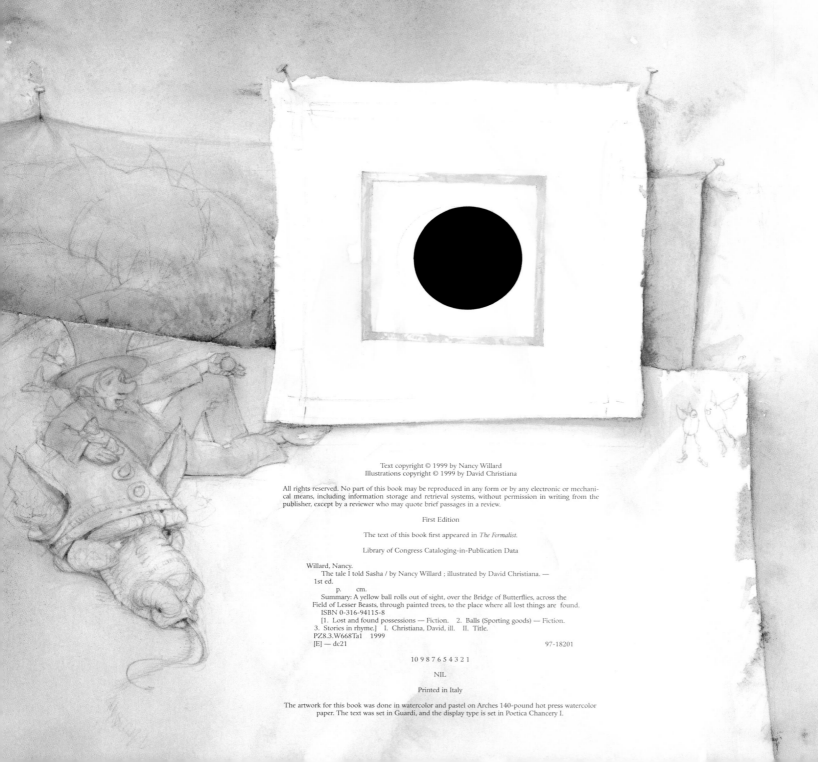

For Sasha, who heard the
story first

N.W

Every color, mark, and
wish is for Harley

D. C.

Text copyright © 1999 by Nancy Willard
Illustrations copyright © 1999 by David Christiana

First Edition

The text of this book first appeared in *The Formalist*.

Library of Congress Cataloging-in-Publication Data

Willard, Nancy.
 The tale I told Sasha / by Nancy Willard ; illustrated by David Christiana. —
1st ed.
        p.   cm.
 Summary: A yellow ball rolls out of sight, over the Bridge of Butterflies, across the
Field of Lesser Beasts, through painted trees, to the place where all lost things are found.
 ISBN 0-316-94115-8
 [1. Lost and found possessions — Fiction.   2. Balls (Sporting goods) — Fiction.
3. Stories in rhyme.]   I. Christiana, David, ill.   II. Title.
 PZ8.3.W668Ta1   1999
 [E] — dc21   97-18201

10 9 8 7 6 5 4 3 2 1

NIL

Printed in Italy

The artwork for this book was done in watercolor and pastel on Arches 140-pound hot press watercolor
paper. The text was set in Guardi, and the display type is set in Poetica Chancery I.

"Why, sometimes I've believed as many as six impossible things before breakfast."
— The White Queen, THROUGH THE LOOKING-GLASS

Mother gave me a yellow ball
because the day was wet and dull.
Our dining room was dark and plain.
Our living room was plain and small.

Our mantel clock did not keep time
but in the thinning evening light
its shadow deepened to a door
that opened nearly out of sight

on brighter rooms, an older space.
The yellow ball bounced here and there.
I chased it through the painted trees
but could not find it anywhere.
A boy with a red balloon
told me he'd seen it heading east,

over the Bridge of Butterflies,
across the Field of Lesser Beasts.
"All winged travelers must walk.
All those with wheels get to ride."
He did not warn me of the web
that shimmered on the other side.

"I gather cows and coins," it sang,
"and travelers from the western shore."

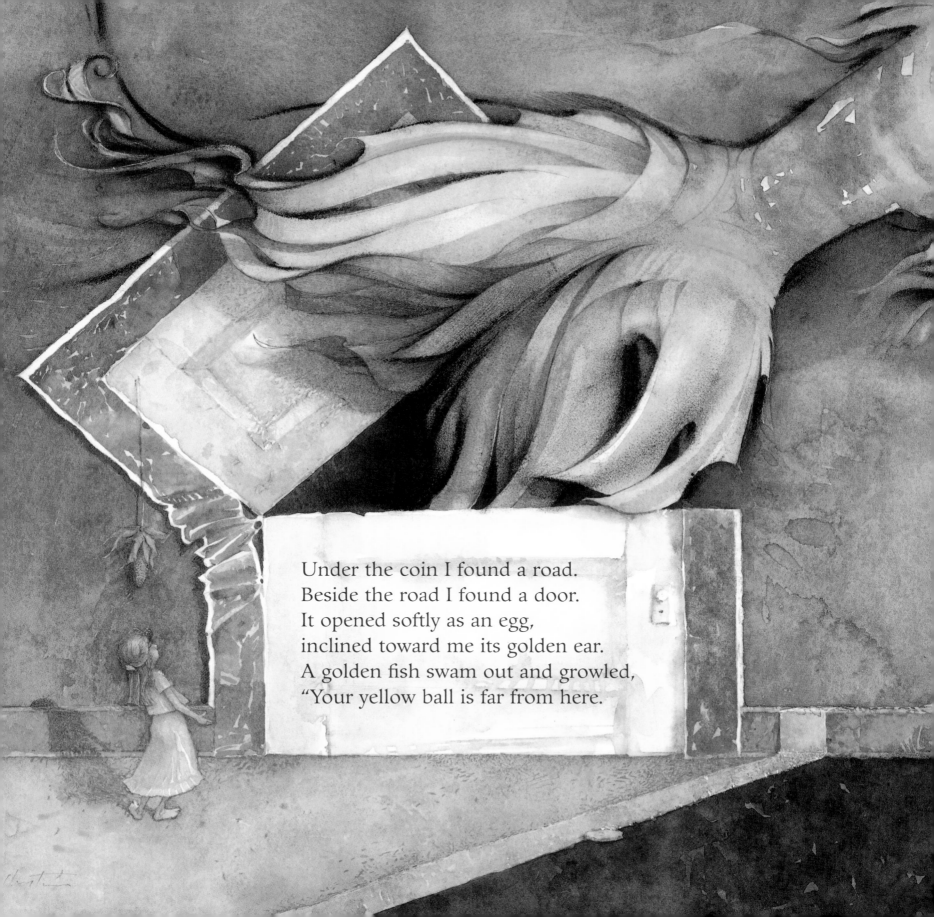

Under the coin I found a road.
Beside the road I found a door.
It opened softly as an egg,
inclined toward me its golden ear.
A golden fish swam out and growled,
"Your yellow ball is far from here.

"A farmer planted it and hoped
for flowers gold as finch's wings
that might attract the Spotted Beast
and other rare delightful things —
a golden horse, a golden hen,
a honey-colored harlequin,
the jewel-winged beetle bearing home
his twilight sherbet, pansy creams,
and starlight-covered jelly beans.

"The farmer is the King of Keys.
Pebbles, velvets, whistles, bees,
whatever comes here comes to him,
mushroom, thimble, mandolin,
thin or furry, straight or sweet.
Slip this map beneath your feet."

Before I'd traveled half a block
I spied the needle Mother dropped
(mending my dress two nights before —
we'd searched for hours on the floor),
the card that always disappears
(we haven't played Old Maid for years),

pennies I'd carried in my shoes,
the silver dimes I always lose,
bread crusts I'd hidden, hard as wood,
the puzzle pieces gone for good,
things worn or wished on, old or lost,
roses astonished by the frost,
the snails and numbers, stars and sheep
my mother counts to fall asleep.

A steamship gleamed on painted seas

and at its helm the King of Keys
(a sleeping tiger at his heels)
was singing what a sailor feels
when everything he loves is lost.
"By all the beasts I haven't caught
and all the wars I've never fought,
by birds and words, by shells and bells,
by time, the master of us all,
I give you back your yellow ball."

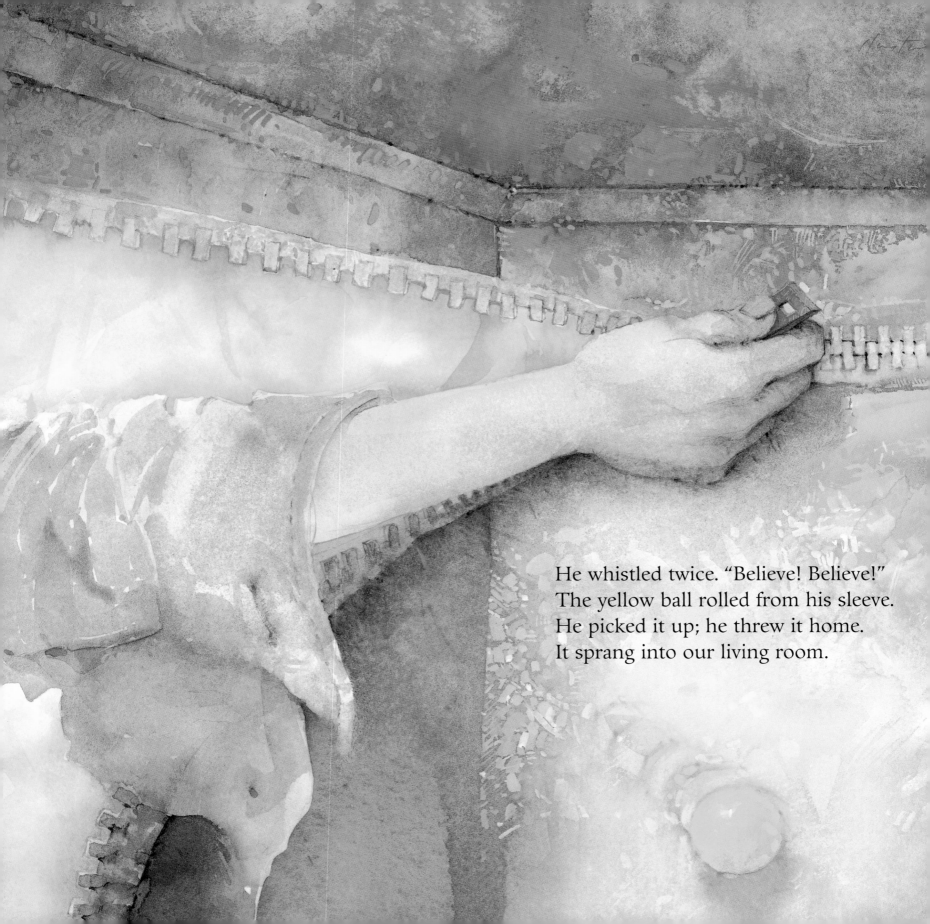

He whistled twice. "Believe! Believe!"
The yellow ball rolled from his sleeve.
He picked it up; he threw it home.
It sprang into our living room.

Our house is quiet, small and plain,
and yet its rooms run far and wide.
A hundred pencils, swift as rain,
writing on sheets of beaten gold
would not be quick enough to hold
the strange adventures

shadows hide.